THE NEW BABY AND ME!

Copyright © Tiny Owl Publishing 2018
Text © Christine Kidney 2018
Illustrations © Hoda Haddadi 2018

First published in the UK in 2018 by Tiny Owl Publishing, London
First published in the US in 2020 by Tiny Owl Publishing, London

www.tinyowl.co.uk

CIP record of this book is available from the Library of Congress.

ISBN 978-1-910328-65-1

Printed in China

THE NEW BABY AND ME!

Christine Kidney • Hoda Haddadi

TINY OWL

Our baby brother is arriving soon.
We have been thinking about him.

A lot.

What will he be like?

My baby brother will
be an explorer,

just like me.

We will find new lands
and rare beasts.

My baby brother will be a scientist,

just like me.

We will look and think,
and discover.

My baby brother
will be an artist,

just like me.

We will paint the world
inside and outside.

My baby brother will be a pirate,

just like me.

We will sail the high seas for treasure.

My baby brother will be a dreamer,

just like me.

We will stare out of the window
and wonder.

What a surprise!

Our baby brother is...

... a girl!

What will she be like?

Our baby sister is a little like us,

but mostly she is...
just like herself!

CREATE A COLLAGE
with HODA HADDADI

Hoda Haddadi is an award-winning artist from Iran. In this book, Hoda creates her illustrations using collage. Collage is when you use lots of old bits of paper or material to create something new.

Creating beautiful artwork can be a fun way to celebrate your new brother or sister. Here are some ideas from Hoda for you to try with your grown-up:

 Design a 'Welcome Home' sign for the new baby from bits of old paper, material or wrapping paper and hang it on the wall for the new baby to look at.

 Create a 'New Baby and Me' collage using material, paper, photos and paint to stamp your footprints or handprints.

 Make a 'New Baby and Me' scrapbook. Where were you born? How much did you weigh? Who was your first visitor? Design one page for the new baby and one page for you.

For more ideas and worksheets visit www.tinyowl.co.uk